JAMES

PERCY

Based on *The Railway Series* by the Rev. W. Awdry

Photographs by David Mitton and Terry Permane for Britt Allcroft's producti
of *Thomas the Tank Engine and Friends*.

First American Edition, 1993.
Copyright © by William Heinemann Ltd. 1991. Photographs copyright © by Britt Allcr
(Thomas) Ltd. 1986. All rights reserved under International and Pan-American Copyrig
Conventions. Published in the United States by Random House, Inc., New York.
Originally published in Great Britain by Buzz Books, an imprint of Reed International
Books Ltd., London. All publishing rights: William Heinemann Ltd., London. All
television and merchandising rights licensed by William Heinemann Ltd. to Britt Allcro
(Thomas) Ltd. exclusively, worldwide.

Library of Congress Cataloging-in-Publication Data
Thomas and Trevor / [photographs by David Mitton and Terry Permane for Britt Allcrof
production of Thomas the Tank Engine and friends]. —1st American ed.   p. . cm.
"Based on The Railway series by the Rev. W. Awdry"—Verso t.p.   "Originally publishe
in Great Britain by Buzz Books"—Verso t.p.   SUMMARY: Trevor, a Traction Engine, is
happy that he can be useful when he helps Thomas with his work at the harbor.
ISBN 0–679–84766–9 (trade)   [1. Railroads—Trains—Fiction.]
I. Mitton, David, ill.   II. Permane, Terry, ill. III. Awdry, W.   Railway series.
IV. Thomas the Tank Engine and friends.
PZ7.T36946 1993   [E]—dc20   92-43774

Manufactured in Great Britain   10 9 8 7 6 5 4 3 2 1

Random House, Inc.   New York, Toronto, London, Sydney, Auckland

THOMAS AND TREVOR

Random 🏠 House

Trevor the Traction Engine enjoys living in the
vicarge orchard on the Island of Sodor.
Edward the Blue Engine once helped to save
him from being turned into scrap, so now
Trevor lives at the vicarage and the two
engines are great friends.

Edward comes to see Trevor every day.
Sometimes Trevor is sad because he doesn't
have enough work to do.

8

"I do like to keep busy all the time," Trevor sighed one day, "and I do like company, especially children's company."

9

"Cheer up," smiled Edward. "Sir Topham Hatt has work for you at his new harbor—I'm to take you to meet Thomas today."

"Oh!" exclaimed Trevor happily. "A harbor, the seaside, children—that will be lovely."

Trevor's freight car was coupled behind
Edward, and they set off to meet Thomas.

Thomas was on his way to the harbor with a
trainload of metal pilings. They were needed
to make the harbor wall firm and safe.

"Hello, Thomas," said Edward. "This is Trevor, a friend of mine. He's a Traction Engine."

Thomas eyed the newcomer doubtfully. "A *what* engine?" he asked.

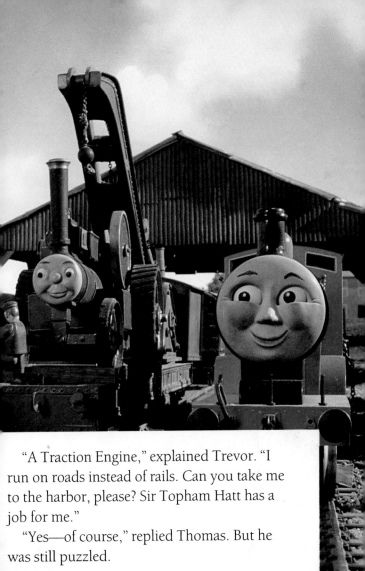

"A Traction Engine," explained Trevor. "I run on roads instead of rails. Can you take me to the harbor, please? Sir Topham Hatt has a job for me."

"Yes—of course," replied Thomas. But he was still puzzled.

Workmen coupled Trevor's freight car to Thomas's train, and soon they were ready to start their journey.

"I'm glad Sir Topham Hatt needs me,"

called Trevor. "I don't have enough to do sometimes, you know, although I can work anywhere—in orchards, on farms, in scrapyards, even at harbors."

"But you don't run on rails," puffed Thomas.

"I'm a Traction Engine—I don't need rails to be useful," replied Trevor. "You wait and see."

When they reached the harbor, they found everything in confusion. Freight cars had been derailed, blocking the line, and stone slabs lay everywhere.

"We must get these pilings through," said Thomas's driver. "They are essential. Trevor," he said, "we need you to drag them round this mess."

"Just the sort of job I like," replied Trevor. "Now you'll see, Thomas—I'll soon show you what Traction Engines can do."

Trevor was as good as his word. First he dragged the stones clear with chains. Then he towed the pilings into position.

"Who needs rails?" he muttered cheerfully to himself.

Later Thomas brought his two coaches, Annie and Clarabel, to visit Trevor.

Thomas was most impressed. "Now I understand how useful a Traction Engine can be," he said.

Thomas's coaches were full of children, and Trevor gave them rides along the harbor. Of all the jobs he did at the harbor that day, he liked this best of all.

"He's very kind," said Annie.

"He reminds me of Thomas," added Clarabel.

24

Everyone was sorry when it was time for
Trevor to go. Thomas pulled him to the
junction.

A small tear came into Trevor's eye. Thomas pretended not to see and whistled gaily to make Trevor happy.

"I'll come and see you if I can," Thomas promised. "The Vicar will look after you, and

there's plenty of work for you now at the orchard, but we may need you again at the harbor someday."

"That would be wonderful," said Trevor happily.

That evening, Trevor stood in the orchard remembering his new friend, Thomas, the harbor, and—most of all—the children. Then he went happily to sleep in the shed at the bottom of the orchard.

THOMAS

EDWAR

GORDON